The Art of Tiny Tales

Jane Garrett

Cover Art by Christian Reid

INNOVATIVE
LEARNING PRESS

Edited by Gracie York
Cover art by Christian Reid

Innovative Learning Press
Apache Junction, AZ
www.innovativepress.org

Acknowledgments

Thank you to all my students. You have inspired me to write these workbooks and supplemental journals. Your enthusiasm for writing sparked the desire in me to make sure you have all the tools you need to become a young author.

I want to thank The Writer's Block—the amazing team of writers from Johns Hopkins University. I would not have been able to get this workbook to market without the Blockheads. Thank you Shayna, Monica, Peyton, Doug, and Daniel. A special shout out to Jay Daniels, just a typical "guy" who wrote a story for me to share. Thank you for contributing so much of your time to this project.

I want to thank my kiddos, Emma and Christian, for all the unwavering support and believing that mom could do anything. Even though you are now "grown," you still believe I am a superhero. I love you for that. Christian, you are the most talented artist I know. Without your inspirational cover designs, no one would even look at my books. Emma, you've got some mad editing skills, girl. I wonder where you learned that from.

Most of all, thank you Captain Awesome! You have always believed in me and your support is the main reason I continued to torture myself week after week, hunched over my computer. Remember when you told me it would be worth it? As sometimes happens, you were right. You cleaned house, scrounged dinner, walked the dog, did the dishes, and made sure I had everything I needed to complete this project. I would not have been able to accomplish this without your full support. I am so glad you married me.

Table Of Contents

Did You Know?

A Magical Journey Through Flash Fiction: The Art of Tiny Tales

In this journey, you'll discover how to craft powerful narratives that fit within a few hundred words, sharpening your skills in creativity, precision, and imagination. Flash fiction challenges you to distill big ideas—emotions, characters, and plots— into a tiny yet impactful package, offering a fresh way to explore the art of writing. Get ready to unleash your inner author and see how much story you can pack into a single, fleeting moment!

Using this Workbook

This workbook is set up so that you can learn, brainstorm, make mistakes, and create amazing stories. The first chapter will give you some helpful advice for writing Flash Fiction stories.

The first section of this workbook is a brief overview of basic writing information with specifics about Flash Fiction. If you have not had creative writing classes before, some of it may be a little confusing.

On the Table of Contents, I have provided you with a place to fill in your title after you have written your story.

The following pages are included to offer some additional help:

Sample Worksheets

There is a sample flash fiction and the corresponding story worksheets filled out as an example of how you can effectively utilize the writing worksheets provided.

Writing Prompts

We have supplied plenty of writing prompts for you to choose from, or you can skip them and brainstorm your own story ideas. These are primarily focused on fantasy and adventure themes.

In each writing section, you'll find the following:

- » Research Worksheet
- » Worldbuilding Worksheet
- » Character Worksheets
- » Conflict Worksheet
- » Story Timeline (Outline)
- » Lined Pages

Short and Sweet

Flash fiction is a super short form of storytelling, typically ranging from a few words to a maximum of 1,500 words, though most pieces land between 300 and 500. It's all about packing a complete story—beginning, middle, and end—into a tiny package. Think of it like a quick punch: it hits fast, leaves an impression, and doesn't linger too long. Because of its brevity, every word counts, and there's no room for fluff. Writers often use it to experiment with ideas, play with structure, or capture a single, sharp moment.

The key to writing flash fiction is focus. You've got to zero in on one idea, character, or scene and make it pop without sprawling into a longer narrative. It's less about explaining everything and more about suggesting—just enough to spark the reader's imagination. A strong opening grabs attention right away, and the ending often twists, surprises, or lingers in a way that feels satisfying despite the short length. It's like a snapshot, not a full movie.

Economy is your best friend here. You're trimming fat—cutting extra descriptions, backstory, or dialogue that doesn't pull its weight. Writers often lean on vivid images or a single, strong emotion to carry the piece. For example, instead of describing a whole rainy day, you might focus on the sound of boots squelching in a puddle to hint at the mood. The challenge is saying a lot with a little, which makes it both tricky and fun.

Common approaches include starting in the middle of the action, this is referred to as "media res." You don't have to end a flash fiction with the same level of closure that you would for some other longer stories. In fact, some feel like tiny mysteries, others like fleeting memories. You may even read a flash fiction where the ending feels like a bit of a cliffhanger, but there's enough inference that you understand what happens.

One thing about reading flash fiction is that whatever the style, the goal is to leave the reader feeling something—amused, unsettled, or curious—in just a handful of sentences. It's a great way to practice precision and test your storytelling chops.

Elements of Story

There are five main elements to every story. Here is a brief overview:

Plot

The plot is what happens in your story. To be clear, a Flash Fiction piece is a complete story. Just like a longer piece of fiction, your piece needs a beginning, a middle, and an ending. Every great story has a problem to solve or a challenge to overcome. The plot is what your character wants or needs to happen and what he or she goes through to get it. Since this type of story is short, keep your plot simple.

Character

Often referred to as the protagonist or main character, they are the hero of their own story. Your character is the heart of your story. They can be brave, funny, kind, or mischievous – anything you dream up! Let them come to life in the reader's mind. If your readers don't care about your character, they won't care about the story.

Setting

The setting is not just the location and time of your story. The setting helps us understand your characters, their lives, culture, and their history. In fantasy and sci-fi, this is referred to as worldbuilding. You will need to use strong, short sentences to establish the setting in Flash Fiction.

Theme

Most often, a story's theme is a broader message or lesson about life. The lesson the main character learns may seem unimportant when weighed against the other elements. However, just like in life, the lessons learned are what gives the story meaning.

Point of View

An author's point of view (POV) is the perspective or angle from which a story is told. It's the author's special way of seeing and sharing the events, emotions, and thoughts of the characters in their tale. Just like looking through different windows will show you different angles of the world outside your house, an author's POV determines how a story is told and what information the author shares with the reader.

To help you select your POV, let's discuss each one: first person, second person, and third person limited or omniscient.

First Person POV:

In first person POV stories, the narrator is usually one of the characters in the story. The narrator tells the story using words like "I" and "me" to share their experiences and feelings. It's like having a friend tell you all about their exciting adventure. For example:

"I woke up early in the morning, and the sun's warm rays streamed through my window. I knew today was going to be a day full of surprises!"

Second Person POV:

Second person POV is like writing your story to a specific person. The narrator uses the word "you" to make it seem like they're speaking directly to you, the reader. It is the least popular POV but done well, it can be a fun way to read a story . For example:

"You walk through the enchanted forest, and the trees whisper secrets as you pass by. You wonder how it all came to this point, when even the trees gossiped behind your back."

Third Person POV:

In a story told from the third person POV, the narrator is an outside observer rather than one of the characters. They use words like "he," "she," and "they" to describe what the characters are doing and feeling. It's like watching a movie unfold in your mind. There are two types of third person POV:

Third Person Limited:

The narrator focuses on the thoughts and feelings of one main character, giving you a deeper understanding of their emotions. For example:

"Samantha tiptoed through the haunted house, her heart pounding loudly in her chest. She wondered if she would find the hidden treasure before the ghostly clock struck midnight."

Third Person Omniscient:

The narrator knows the thoughts and feelings of multiple characters and can share different perspectives through-out the story. For example:

"As the sun set over the magical kingdom, the princess and the brave knight prepared for the epic battle. Little did they know that a mischievous fairy was watching, ready to intervene and change their fate."

Each type of POV gives a unique flavor to a story, and authors choose the one that best fits the tale they want to tell. So, the next time you read a book, pay attention to the author's POV, and you'll see how it adds depth and excitement to the story.

Research

Fiction is an illusion. It's a made-up tale of something that never happened, and it's your job as the author to get readers to accept that illusion. Readers need to feel like the story is real, or they will not emotionally connect with it. If the world you've built or the characters you've crafted don't ring true, the whole thing falls apart—readers will sense the cracks and lose interest. Your task is to pull them in so completely that they forget they're holding a book, and that starts with making every detail feel authentic.

They say to write what you know. But I say, unless you are writing about a kid that doesn't like school or struggles with chores and siblings, you are going to have to learn about the world your character is living in. Most stories stretch beyond your own backyard—whether it's a medieval village, a distant planet, or a high-stakes courtroom drama. Depending on the world you are creating or the adventure your character is going on, you may have to do research. That's not a chore; it's a chance to deepen your story and make it stand up to scrutiny.

Research is worth the time to ensure that you can create believable characters and actions. You will use research on anything, including history, maps, weather reports, cultural behaviors, language, clothing, weapons, and more. Writing a pirate tale? You'll need to know how ships work and what the crew eats. Crafting a sci-fi epic? You might dig into theories about space travel or alien ecosystems. These details aren't just background noise—they shape how your characters move, speak, and think, grounding the illusion in something solid.

The effort pays off when readers buy into your world without hesitation. A warrior wielding a sword wrong or a desert town with impossible rain can jolt them out of the story. Research helps you avoid those missteps, letting you focus on the heart of the tale—your characters and their struggles. So, dig into the facts, weave them into your fiction, and watch the illusion come alive. It's the difference between a story that's skimmed and one that's remembered.

Character

Often referred to as the "protagonist," your main character is so much more. He is a human being—or at least feels like one—with habits, desires, fears, quirks, weaknesses, and strengths. These traits are what make readers identify with him and, ultimately, care about him. Creating a truly dimensional character is the backbone of your novel. If readers don't care about your character, don't like him, or can't connect with him in some way, then they won't care about the rest of the story. The story goal, other characters, the epic battle, or falling in love—none of it will matter if the protagonist doesn't click with the audience. I will use some examples from popular animated movies. Let's start with Simba from *The Lion King*—his curiosity, grief over losing his father, and determination to reclaim his rightful place in the pride make him someone kids root for.

For your story, especially when writing for kids, it's important to remember that young readers are simple and generally straightforward thinkers. They care about characters they know, identify with, or sympathize with. Think about the people in your family or your friends—those are the ones whose lives you wonder about. Now compare that to the person who took your order at a restaurant or the random people in the library. You don't really care about their lives or what kind of day they're having because you don't know them at all. In *Moana*, kids connect with Moana because she's restless and brave, dreaming of adventure beyond her island—just like they might dream of something bigger in their own lives.

This isn't because you're selfish or mean—it's just how humans work. We care about the people we know, the ones we feel attached to. This attachment isn't the same as sympathy or empathy; it's deeper. It's about caring enough to be concerned about what happens in someone's daily life, not just feeling sorry for them in a tough moment. In *Toy Story*, Woody's loyalty to Andy and his jealousy over Buzz Lightyear make him relatable—kids know what it's like to feel left out or protective of something they love. That connection keeps them invested in whether Woody finds his way back home.

A strong protagonist gives kids a reason to stay with the story. If your character feels flat or distant, the plot—no matter how exciting—won't hold their attention. Look at Elsa in *Frozen*: her struggle with her powers and her love for Anna make her more than just a magical princess. Kids see her fear of being different and her drive to protect her sister, and that pulls them in. Build a character with layers—flaws, hopes, and all—and you've got the heart of a story that kids won't put down. Without that, even the wildest adventure falls flat.

> **List some of your favorite characters from movies or books and what made them so memorable for you?**

Conflict

The harder the conflict, the more glorious the triumph. —Martin Luther King.

"To live is to war with trolls." —Henrik Ibsen

One thing is for sure—no one really likes conflict. So, why is it important to have conflict in stories? Because at the heart of fiction is conflict. If your main character is not clashing with the villain, nature, or even himself, then it is boring. If there are no battles to be fought and the evil king is willing to just stay inside his castle and nap all day, then what is the point of the story? Readers need something to root for, a reason to care about what happens next. Conflict gives the story purpose and keeps it moving forward.

Conflict should be in every chapter and every scene. Whether that conflict is external or internal, it needs to be present to entice the reader to turn the page and see what happens next. It doesn't have to be a really big conflict—there are small conflicts as well, and we will discuss those soon. External conflicts might involve a fight with an enemy or a struggle against a storm, while internal conflicts could be a character wrestling with guilt or fear. Both types work together to build tension and hold the reader's interest.

Fortunately, conflict is not too difficult to write. Think about the last time you got into an argument with your brother or sister, or even an argument with a good friend. How hard was that to escalate? Not very hard. All you have to do is write in obstacles to stop your character from attaining his goal at the end of the story. Heap on misery, betrayal, and injury. Go for it—it's good for him, and your readers will love you for it! The more challenges you throw at your character, the more chances they get to grow and surprise the audience.

So, why would you create a character that readers care about, then subject him to such continuous torture? Simple. Without conflict, he would have no reason to exist. He certainly would not be a hero. A character who sails through life with no problems doesn't earn the title of hero—heroes are forged through struggle. Conflict shapes them, tests them, and gives them a chance to prove who they are. Readers connect with that journey.

Now, let's talk about those small conflicts. Not every scene needs a fire-breathing dragon attacking attacking the peaceful village or even a shouting match between co-workers. Small conflicts can be just as effective—maybe the character forgets an important detail, or a friend misunderstands their intentions. These little hurdles add layers to the story and keep the pace steady. They also make the bigger conflicts feel earned, building up to those moments when everything is on the line. Mixing small and large conflicts creates a rhythm that keeps readers engaged.

In the end, conflict is the engine of fiction. It drives the plot, reveals character, and gives the story stakes. Without it, there's no tension, no growth, and no reason for anyone to keep reading. So, embrace it—let your characters stumble, fight, and claw their way through. That's where the real story happens, and that's what turns a blank page into something worth reading. Conflict isn't just important; it's essential.

Worldbuilding

The setting of a story is often called the storyworld, and this term fits especially well for fantasy or sci-fi tales. The setting informs everything else in the story—it's the foundation that shapes the plot, characters, and even the stakes. It's how readers can best "see" your characters throughout the story, picturing where they stand, what they face, and how their surroundings influence their actions. A strong setting doesn't just sit there; it pulls readers in and makes the whole narrative feel alive.

The setting is not just the location and time of your story, though those pieces matter. They're only a fraction of this element. The setting encompasses the entire storyworld—every layer of the environment your characters inhabit. This includes the geography, weather, and architecture, but also the culture, history, traditions, and daily routines that define life there. The setting helps us understand your characters: their lives, how they dress and speak, what they value, and what motivates them. In a sci-fi story, a gritty space station might explain a character's toughness, while a lush fantasy forest might tie to their deep connection to nature.

How you build and relate your storyworld has a direct effect on your reader's experience. A vague or sloppy setting can leave readers confused or detached, while a well-crafted one keeps them hooked. The setting is a moving, changing, exciting part of your story— it's not static. A city might bustle with trade one day and burn in a siege the next. Making sure that your storyworld is realistic and interesting is about details. Every choice, from the food on a character's plate to the sound of a distant storm, builds trust in the world you've created and deepens the reader's investment.

Brainstorming, researching, and taking notes as you build your world are very important steps to the process of writing a fictional story. Start with the basics: Where is this place? When does it happen? Then dig deeper—sketch out the rules of the society, the technology or magic at play, and the history that shaped it. Research can fill in gaps, whether it's studying medieval farming for a fantasy village or planetary orbits for a sci-fi epic. Notes keep it all straight, so your world stays consistent. A detailed, thoughtful storyworld doesn't just support your characters—it becomes a character itself, driving the story forward.

Some Advice for Writing Flash Fiction:

» Start in the middle of the action. You don't have time for a long buildup. Just "drop" your reader into the exciting part.

» Stick to one event. Focus on one particular moment in time. You should show one or two scenes at most.

» Work with just one or two characters. You don't have time to develop a whole cast. It's better to have one or two strong characters than a bunch that the reader cannot keep track of.

» Write strong descriptions. Make every single word count. Help your readers visualize as much as possible.

» Use strong titles. Titles can do a lot for your story. They can hook the reader as well as anchor your story and do some worldbuilding. For example, a title like "The Dragon Guild: Invasion of the Loridia Kingdom," does some character and worldbuilding before your story even starts.

» Try first person point of view. This will create an instant connection to the reader and allow you to express more in fewer words.

» Give the readers a good twist and turn. Give them what they expect, but in an unexpected way. They expect the main character to achieve something, but they want to be surprised by how that happens. Creating surprise is what Flash Fiction is all about; take the reader on a journey, no matter how short.

» Begin with a bang. In Flash Fiction, the opening sentence is like a magical door that invites readers into your story. Make it catchy and exciting to hook your readers from the very beginning.

» Flash fiction endings do not always need to be all neat and tidy or wrapped up in with a bow. Your readers have an imagination of their own. Feel free to pique their imagination with a little bit of mystery.

One of the best ways to learn how to write flash fiction is by looking at examples. Before I turn you loose with a head spinning with ideas, let's analyze a piece of flash fiction. Read through the flash fiction *The Light*, by Jay Daniels. After the story, I have provided you with notes that highlight the author's intentional use of writing craft.

The Light *by Jay Daniels*

For the first time in her life, Angelica felt uncomfortable and out of place in a ballgown. She usually wore them in carriages on the way to balls, in palaces where balls were in progress, or in lieu of a mantua at the occasional gala. This place was, by the feel of things, a chilly seaside cavern. Rather than soft string music, rushing waves echoed down water-smoothed tunnels. Rather than uncomfortable shoes tapping on polished marble, small crabs chittered and scurried away from the large, perfumed intruder in their rocky home.

And thank the Seraph of Love for that perfume. Angelica could already detect hints of fish in the air. Without the invisible shield of lemon and cloves, she expected retching and dry heaving would be in order.

"Persephone," she called, her voice repeated many times by the echo. "Persephone, I can't see a thing. Can't you glow or something?"

Angelica heard, off to her left, what sounded very much like a panicked court sorcerer sloshing through a pool of water. This was followed a second later by a small gasp of relief and the appearance of dancing golden specks on the ceiling and walls of the cave.

Persephone, also in a gown but one with fewer pearl inlays, was crouched among the silt and flotsam, elbow deep in a murky puddle. The golden light grew brighter, and the refracted pinpricks wheeled about them as she drew her staff free of the muck with a squelch.

"I'm very sorry, my queen," said Persephone, giving the staff a shake to rid it of grime. It was plain, living aspen wood, almost as pale and thin as its wielder, with a dozen yellow leaves sprouting along its upper half. The leaves' internal veins glowed like heated filaments, casting the light of the Seraph upon them.

"As I expected," said Angelica, taking in the dripping stalactites. "Long distance portals are still beyond your skill."

"Yes, your highness. I'm very sorry, your highness."

"I wouldn't have been angry if you told me. And I promise it would have been less upsetting to wait for a more experienced wizard than to end up...any idea where we are?"

"I..." Persephone's eyes darted around the cavern, stopping when they found what appeared to be the only exit, a half-flooded tunnel that curved out of sight after just a few feet. Angelica had marked it as soon as there was enough light to see.

"Persephone!" Angelica clapped her hands, and Persephone squeaked in fright, clutching her staff like a child with a comforting blanket. "Come on, we're not swimming out of here. My dress at least is still salvageable—just trim the hem, maybe leave it short—so portal us back to our castle."

"Of course, my queen, right away." But Persephone made no move to begin inscribing a circle, nor to chant, nor to consult her handbook. Her gaze remained fixed on that tunnel.

Angelica huffed. "Oh please, girl, if you're worried about punishment, don't be. When we were your age, Lady Belmont herself dropped us into Prince Sabian's moat. He fills it with sewage—and she still became Mistress of the Kiln or Lady of the Fireplace." She waved a dismissive hand. "However you all address the big witch these days. So, hop to it. Let's see some sparkles."

Persephone did not have a chance to reply, because, at that moment, the singing began. It was faint at first, fighting with the sound of the waves. Once Angelica took a moment to listen, however, it quickly drowned out all else. The tone and rhythm were that of a jolly tavern bard, but the voice could have moved the imperial opera house to tears.

"To drown, to drown, the sailors fear,

"A frown, A frown, that's all I hear,

"Will split the face of ev'ry man,

"Who meets a siren far from land,

"Yet ev'ry time we drag one down,

"Tis ever a smile and never a frown.

"Oh-la-da-da, oh-hi-dee-dee, a siren's kiss makes liars of thee."

From around the bend in the tunnel came a small figure, a head shorter than Angelica, skipping on the surface of the water. Her black hair was longer than her whole body and fanned out on the ripples behind her. She wore no clothes, that Angelica could see, but was covered in so much salt, sand, and seaweed that the court ladies would have mocked her as overly modest. She gave a twirl as she stepped into the cavern, dropping the words but humming the same tune, and raised a hand to shield her eyes from Persephone's staff.

"Halt there, daemon," said Angelica, thrusting her palm forward. "You may not step into the light of the Seraph."

The girl did halt, fingers still covering her eyes and throwing her face into shadow, but her mouth had split into a grin. She spoke, and somehow the humming never stopped. "Sephy-y-y! Put the light out! You know it hurts!"

The light did not go out, but flared. The siren hissed and recoiled. Angelica turned to Persephone and saw a ring of blazing gold beside her. Through it was a frozen forest under a bright blue sky. "Where—never mind," Angelica fixed her eyes on the siren again, hiked up her gown, and backed toward the portal. "Close it as soon as—"

"My queen," said Persephone, sounding much more distant than a moment ago, "I'm very sorry." And the light went out.

Angelica blinked in the total dark. "P-P-Persephone?" But the sorceress had gone.

Around her, the song began again, and there were many more voices singing.

ANALYSIS: The Light *by Jay Daniels*

For the first time in her life, Angelica felt uncomfortable and out of place in a ballgown. It's good practice to establish POV early in flash fiction so readers have as much time as possible to connect with your character, despite how short the stories are. She usually wore them in carriages on the way to balls, in palaces where balls were in progress, or in lieu of a mantua at the occasional gala. This place was, by the feel of things, a chilly seaside cavern. Rather than soft string music, rushing waves echoed down water-smoothed tunnels. Rather than uncomfortable shoes tapping on polished marble, small crabs chittered and scurried away from the large, perfumed intruder in their rocky home. Because flash fiction is so short, you need to establish what is abnormal or out of place from the very start. This is the first building block of conflict.

And thank the Seraph of Love for that perfume. Angelica could already detect hints of fish in the air. Without the invisible shield of lemon and cloves, she expected retching and dry heaving would be in order. This paragraph serves two purposes. The first sentence does a bit of worldbuilding, letting us know that our character believes in someone or something. There rest expands the senses the readers can use to experience the story.

"Persephone," she called, her voice repeated many times by the echo. "Persephone, I can't see a thing. Can't you glow or something?"

Angelica heard, off to her left, what sounded very much like a panicked court sorcerer sloshing through a pool of water. This was followed a second later by a small gasp of relief and the appearance of dancing golden specks on the ceiling and walls of the cave. There's not a lot of room for character introductions in flash fiction. You get maybe a paragraph for an intro. Anything else has to be woven into the action of the story.

Persephone, also in a gown but one with fewer pearl inlays, was crouched among the silt and flotsam, elbow deep in a murky puddle. The golden light grew brighter, and the refracted pinpricks wheeled about them as she drew her staff free of the muck with a squelch. Here is the first display of magic. Here again, flash fiction does not allow for lots of explaining and complex systems. Almost everything has to be part of the story's action.

"I'm very sorry, my queen," said Persephone, This dialogue tells us a bit more about Angelica (that she's a queen) and Persephone (that the situation they're in is her fault). giving the staff a shake to rid it of grime. It was plain, living aspen wood, almost as pale and thin as its wielder, with a dozen yellow leaves sprouting along its upper half. The leaves' internal veins glowed like heated filaments, casting the light of the Seraph upon them. The rest of this paragraph is worldbuilding. There is room for a couple of sentences showing off the fantastical elements of the story. It's meant to entertain after all.

"As I expected," said Angelica, taking in the dripping stalactites. "Long distance portals are still beyond your skill."

"Yes, your highness. I'm very sorry, your highness."

"I wouldn't have been angry if you told me. And I promise it would have been less upsetting to wait for a more experienced wizard than to end up...any idea where we are?" The main purpose of this dialogue is to cement the relationship of servant and queen, but also establish that Angelica is not a bad ruler. She's quite understanding and forgiving, considering the circumstances.

"I..." Persephone's eyes darted around the cavern, stopping when they found what appeared to be the only exit, a half-flooded tunnel that curved out of sight after just a few feet. This is the next building block of conflict. They're trapped in an unknown location with only one way out. Angelica had marked it as soon as there was enough light to see.

"Persephone!" Angelica clapped her hands, and Persephone squeaked in fright, clutching her staff like a child with a comforting blanket. Here we cement the idea that Persephone is nervous or scared about what's happening, despite Angelica seeming unconcerned. This is one more block of potential conflict on the pile. "Come on, we're not swimming out of here. My dress at least is still salvageable—just trim the hem, maybe leave it short—so portal us back to our castle."

"Of course, my queen, right away." But Persephone made no move to begin inscribing a circle, nor to chant, nor to consult her handbook. Her gaze remained fixed on that tunnel. Here, we're about halfway through the story, right where I like to show things are going to take a turn toward good or ill fortune. We've established already that Angelica is in charge, she's the queen, so Persephone defying her orders, despite Persephone herself being scared, should set off the first alarms for readers.

Angelica huffed. "Oh please, girl, if you're worried about punishment, don't be. When we were your age, Lady Belmont herself dropped us into Prince Sabian's moat. He fills it with sewage—and she still became Mistress of the Kiln or Lady of the Fireplace." She waved a dismissive hand. "However you all address the big witch these days. So, hop to it. Let's see some sparkles." This deepens Angelica's character. She's not just a generic queen. She's lived a whole life, which we imply by showing just a snippet of here.

Persephone did not have a chance to reply, because, at that moment, the singing began. It was faint at first, fighting with the sound of the waves. Once Angelica took a moment to listen, however, it quickly drowned out all else. The tone and rhythm were that of a jolly tavern bard, but the voice could have moved the imperial opera house to tears.

"To drown, to drown, the sailors fear,

"A frown, A frown, that's all I hear,

"Will split the face of ev'ry man,

"Who meets a siren far from land, This is the most important line from the song. The rest of it lets us know that the singer has some ill intentions, but this line brings it home. We're using all the established mythology around sirens to lend our story a sense of dread.

"Yet ev'ry time we drag one down,

"Tis ever a smile and never a frown.

"Oh-la-da-da, oh-hi-dee-dee, a siren's kiss makes liars of thee."

From around the bend in the tunnel came a small figure, a head shorter than Angelica, skipping on the surface of the water. Her black hair was longer than her whole body and fanned out on the ripples behind her. She wore no clothes, that Angelica could see, but was covered in so much salt, sand, and seaweed that the court ladies would have mocked her as overly modest. She gave a twirl as she stepped into the cavern, dropping the words but humming the same tune, and raised a hand to shield her eyes from Persephone's staff. Some quick worldbuilding here. We do the description of the siren as efficiently as possible, and establish that the light in Persephone's staff has an effect on it.

"Halt there, daemon," said Angelica, thrusting her palm forward. "You may not step into the light of the Seraph."

The girl did halt, fingers still covering her eyes and throwing her face into shadow, but her mouth had split into a grin. She spoke, and somehow the humming never stopped. "Phene-e-e! Put the light out! You know it hurts!" This is the moment of dramatic irony, when we reveal to the readers that the siren knows Persephone (by a nickname even, so it's personal), but Angelica still doesn't realize the whole picture. The conflict is at its peak as we realize this might not have been an accidental portal after all.

The light did not go out, but flared. The siren hissed and recoiled. Angelica turned to Persephone and saw a ring of blazing gold beside her. Through it was a frozen forest under a bright blue sky. "Where—never mind," Angelica fixed her eyes on the siren again, hiked up her gown, and backed toward the portal. "Close it as soon as—"

"My queen," said Persephone, sounding much more distant than a moment ago, "I'm very sorry." And the light went out.

Angelica blinked in the total dark. "P-P-Persephone?" But the sorceress had gone. Resolution to the conflict. Angelica is trapped, abandoned by Persephone, and the stuttering dialogue shows now she's the one who's scared.

Around her, the song began again, and there were many more voices singing. What happens next? Well, we know about sirens, both from the popular mythology and the song we put in the story, so the implication is...not great for Angelica. But, we don't need to spell it out entirely.

Using the Worksheets

Worksheets are provided for you for every story. These are your character, worldbuilding, research, and general idea brainstorming pages. Using worksheets to plan your flash fiction story is incredibly helpful because they provide a structured framework to develop ideas efficiently. Flash fiction often has strict word limits, so every sentence must count.

Worksheets help you pinpoint essential elements like the protagonist, setting, and conflict without getting bogged down in unnecessary details. By outlining your story's arc or key moments ahead of time, you are far more likely to have a fictional narrative that holds the reader's attention and leaves a lasting impression, even in a short format.

Additionally, worksheets serve as prompts to spark ideas and even may help you overcome writer's block. This preparatory work saves time during the actual writing process, allowing you to focus on crafting vivid moments and scenes rather than figuring out the events and characters as you write—which often leads to lots and lots of revisions.

Although you will not necessarily use every worksheet completely, they are here to help you filter though the ideas in your head and support them with concrete details that are the foundation for all great stories!

To help you get a better sense of how the worksheets are used, you will read a flash fiction piece titled *Even the air glimmers*, and then review the worksheet samples following the story as a guide for how you might use your worksheets.

Even the Air Glimmers *by Hannah Fouts*

The screen door slammed behind June as she slunk miserably onto the creaky old porch. The cool morning air would do her muddled mind good. She flung herself onto the porch swing taking the book out from under her arm to examine the cover.

Another fantastical extraordinary book read.
Another uneventful ordinary morning.
Another boring normal day being a boring normal girl.

June huffed, tossing her copy of *Alice in Wonderland* to the side. What she'd give to be able to experience the kinds of things that book characters did.

She pulled at a loose thread on her overalls as she looked over the porch railing toward the forest behind her house. She and her sister Maggie used to spend all day out there playing and exploring; Imagining that the impossible wonderful things from the books they read could really happen.

Without letting her mind wander further, June pushed herself to her feet, leaving her novel on the swing and shuffled off the porch towards the woods.

Now that her sister was the mature age of fourteen, she'd spent less and less time in the woods imagining with June. Maggie tried to tell her that she was just too busy worrying about the upcoming freshmen year of high school.

But June knew the truth.

Maggie was getting too old for imagining. June's chest tightened as she stuffed her hands in her pockets. She was already twelve and the thought of being too old to do her favorite thing in the whole world made her feel sick.

Stepping through the treeline, she let out a long breath and took in the scenery that had become so familiar. Everything was always the same in these woods save for a new sprouted plant or an unexpected fallen branch. But as she took it in, she realized that this time, something was different.

A strange light glinted through a patch of clover in a sunny patch of the forest floor. She shot forward, her mind already conjuring up all the wonderful fantastical things it could be. Even though every other time something like this happened, her mysterious glinting light always turned out to be a piece of reflective litter.

June stood over the clover not daring to blink or even breathe. She didn't trust herself to move one little bit in case it was all a strange mirage.

It wasn't litter this time.

She knelt and scooped up a pocket watch. The solid weight of it felt comforting in her hand as she popped open the cover. The quiet tick, tick, tick of the seconds hand assured her even more that this wasn't a figment of her imagination.

A small piece of paper was tangled into the chain of the watch. With trembling fingers, June pulled at the long blue ribbon untying the bow. She smoothed the crinkled paper attempting to make this moment last as long as she could.

> The girl of wonder you were and are
> Will solve this clue even if it's far.
> The place you seek could never be dimmer
> Not when even the air appears to glimmer.

June blinked. Then blinked again convinced that her eyes were playing tricks on her. She'd wanted something like this to happen for years! The prick of excitement couldn't be denied.

What if she had somehow stumbled into the plot of a novel?

June checked herself at the thought. Wasn't she far too old to be entertaining such fantastical notions?

And yet...

Tick, tick, tick.

What if whoever, or whatever, had left this note decided not to stick around for much longer? She needed to solve the riddle. Her mom and sister had left to do the grocery shopping and wouldn't be back for a while. Her dad was at work. No one would know.

Her eyes scanned the beautiful script once more.

The first two lines seemed to be directed at her. Mom used to always say June had wonder in her eyes. Even though she never quite knew what she meant it seemed to be important now. Whoever wrote this clue clearly wanted her to solve it.

Unless there was another "girl of wonder" that she had never met or heard of.

She moved onto the next two lines.

"The place you seek..." June mused to herself. "They must want me to go somewhere."

But what in the world could "*Even the air appears to glimmer*" possibly mean? Her first thought was of the fantasy worlds that seemed to have magic floating in the air like fireflies. That couldn't be right though. The writer—whoever that was—knew that June needed to know how to get there.

She hadn't the faintest idea of how to get to a place like that.

Something kept nagging at her mind though.

Fireflies.

It felt right, but how did it fit with the idea that this place could "*never be dimmer.*" Fireflies only came out in the evening.

Just then it hit her.

A place where the air could always glimmer if light hit it just right.

June took off running. How had she not thought of it before? Of course this would be the place the mysterious clue sent her. It was the most magical place in the whole forest.

About a quarter of a mile into the forest a waterfall spilled over an outcropping of rock into the creek below. To the average onlooker it wouldn't seem like much. Granted the waterfall was only about as tall as June. But to her the waterfall and the clearing around it was magic. She and Maggie used to spend hours there playing, reading, and searching for anything they deemed fantastical.

Her heart beat wildly inside her chest, as the trees whipped past. Anticipation clung to her like the soft mud on the soles of her yellow boots.

The crash of the waterfall met her ears just before she stumbled into the clearing, pushing her wild brown hair out of her face. Looking around her, June searched for whatever the clue might be leading her to. What if she'd solved the clue wrong?.

No, that couldn't be. This had to be the place.

Never in her life had she given up easily and she wasn't about to start now. She stepped carefully towards the water cascading toward the creek below. As it fell and splashed happily, mist flew into the air making the scene around her shimmer with an otherworldly feel.

"Where are you?" June mumbled.

At the base of the waterfall grew a small bush. She and Maggie used to leave little trinkets they wanted to keep safe in there.

Was it possible?

Pushing the branches aside, June caught her breath. At the base of the bush sat the most beautiful journal she'd ever laid eyes on. The cover shimmered just like the air around her with gold leaves and swirling vines.

June picked it up reverently. It was heavier than it looked. Running her hands slowly over the cool smooth cover, she opened it to the first page expecting another clue inside.

The spine gave a satisfying crack as she flipped it open.

A thrill shot up her spine when she saw words written on the inside of the cover. As her eyes moved over them, however, June realized this wasn't just another clue.

Dear June,

I hope you enjoyed the clue that led you here. I knew you read Alice in Wonderland recently, and I wanted to do something special to give this to you.

I'm sorry I haven't been playing with you and spending as much time with you recently. I know it's been hard. But I wanted to let you know that just because I'm growing out of those games doesn't mean you have to.

That's why I'm giving you this journal. Even if you didn't have the woods to imagine in, or even if you were an old lady who couldn't get around, you still have the most important thing. Your sense of wonder with the world.

Now you can write down all the wonderful things you imagine in this journal.

And I can't wait to read them.

Maggie

June pressed her trembling lips together as she held the journal close to her chest. A tear trickled down her cheek as she ran her hands over her sister's handwriting. Even though Maggie was growing up, that didn't mean June couldn't share her stories with her anymore.

It didn't mean she had to give up the thing she loved. Inspiration was all around.

The branches swaying in the breeze.

The glimmering air.

The butterflies flitting from one flower to the next.

Her chest swelled and she wiped her eyes for the final time. With that, June took off toward home. She needed a pen if she were to capture the stories in her head.

The only problem would be deciding which one to write first.

STORY RESEARCH

Research Topic _____

KEY INFORMATION

Genre: MG Contemporary Fiction
Setting: A forested area near June's home, with a waterfall that feels like magic.

STATISTICS & DATA

88% of parents believe their children are growing up too quickly.

LANGUAGE & SLANG

"Slunk" – Describes June's sad, defeated posture.

"Tick, tick, tick" – Mimics the sound of the pocket watch, adding suspense.

Notes

Fireflies are actually beetles, not flies. They produce "cold light" through a chemical reaction called bioluminescence. Their light displays are primarily used for mating. Firefly larvae also glow, and they spend most of their lives in this stage. Not all firefly species flash, some use pheromones. They are found on almost every continent except Antarctica. Fireflies are facing threats from habitat loss, light pollution, and pesticide use.

According to American Rivers, there's a general idea that to be considered a waterfall, a drop should be at least around five feet high.
However, in practical applications like garden water features, much smaller drops are still called waterfalls.

Website Resources Used

UK.GOV for statistics.

WORLDBUILDING

Location

Brief Description

The story takes place in a quiet town surrounded by lush. enchanting forests.The forest is a space for imagination and adventure. brimming with mystery. yet comfortingly constant.

What are the people/Culture like?

June's family is close-knit and supportive. The culture reflects small-town life. where siblings share a deep love for one another despite growing up and changing interests.

How is the climate & Terrain?

The story takes place in a forest. with cool. fresh morning air. The climate is cool and fresh while the terrain contains a creek. and a small waterfall.

Describe using 5 senses

- Sight: A shimmering patch of clover. golden leaves on a journal.
- Sound: The gentle ticking of the watch. the crash of the waterfall.
- Touch: The cool. smooth cover of the journal. the soft moss beneath June's boots.
- Smell: Fresh morning air. earthy scents from the forest.
- Taste: The water at the fall is refreshing and cold.

What do people do all day?

On a typical day. June spends her time in the forest imagining when she isn't at school.

Website Resources Used

Notes

Set the tone for her mood at home from the start. Make sure that contrasts with her mood in the forest.

CHARACTER

Character Name ___June___

Sketch or Paste Image

NickName _____

Physical Description

June is a 12-year-old girl with wild brown hair. bright eyes full of wonder. and a freckled face. She wears worn yellow boots and overalls.

POSITIVE IDEALS

June believes in the magic of imagination. wonder. and adventure .

Personality

June is imaginative. sensitive. and introspective. often lost in thought. She's curious and determined. and nostalgic.

NEGATIVE IDEALS

June struggles with self-doubt.

Habits / Quirks

She pulls at loose threads on her clothes when anxious. gets lost in daydreams. and prefers exploring the forest over mundane activities.

Goals and Motivations

June's goal is to preserve her imagination and to reconnect with her sister.

Background

June used to play in the forest all the time with her older sister. but now things have begun to change. Maggie is growing out of the games they used to play.

CONFLICT

Who is the Conflict between?

The conflict is between June and her sister Maggie. though June is also struggling with internal conflict as well.

What are they having this conflict?

Maggie is getting older and is less interested in the imaginative games she and June used to play in the woods. June is worried that this means it has to happen to her too.

How does the character react internally?

She feels a sense of loss and sadness that Maggie is no longer the partner in imagination she once was. June also felt anxiety about growing up and losing her sense of wonder. that she treasures deeply.

How does the character react externally?

Externally. June reacts by retreating to the woods. which she associates with her shared memories of days spent in the woods with Maggie.

How is the conflict resolved?

The conflict is resolved when June finds the journal left by Maggie. Maggie's letter reassures June that her sense of wonder is a gift she can continue to grow. The journal serves as a reminder to keep imagining and creating.

How does the character change from this conflict?

June changes by learning that growing up doesn't mean giving up the things that bring her joy. like her imagination and sense of wonder.

How does the conflict affect the story?

The conflict drives the plot of the story. Both June's internal and external struggles lead her on a quest to solve the riddle and find the waterfall.

STORY TIMELINE

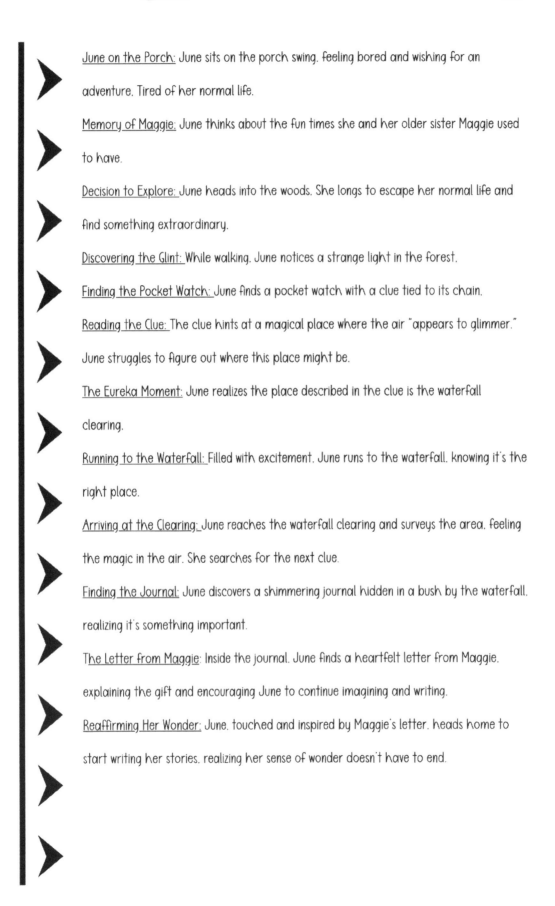

June on the Porch: June sits on the porch swing, feeling bored and wishing for an adventure. Tired of her normal life.

Memory of Maggie: June thinks about the fun times she and her older sister Maggie used to have.

Decision to Explore: June heads into the woods. She longs to escape her normal life and find something extraordinary.

Discovering the Glint: While walking, June notices a strange light in the forest.

Finding the Pocket Watch: June finds a pocket watch with a clue tied to its chain.

Reading the Clue: The clue hints at a magical place where the air "appears to glimmer." June struggles to figure out where this place might be.

The Eureka Moment: June realizes the place described in the clue is the waterfall clearing.

Running to the Waterfall: Filled with excitement, June runs to the waterfall, knowing it's the right place.

Arriving at the Clearing: June reaches the waterfall clearing and surveys the area, feeling the magic in the air. She searches for the next clue.

Finding the Journal: June discovers a shimmering journal hidden in a bush by the waterfall, realizing it's something important.

The Letter from Maggie: Inside the journal, June finds a heartfelt letter from Maggie, explaining the gift and encouraging June to continue imagining and writing.

Reaffirming Her Wonder: June, touched and inspired by Maggie's letter, heads home to start writing her stories, realizing her sense of wonder doesn't have to end.

Flash Fiction Story Prompts:

Once a decade, under the light of the fiery eclipse, a magical carnival comes to the kingdom bringing ethereal delights and one coveted spot for a talented performer to join their troupe. A young musician, an orphan whose hopes are pinned on winning his place, is selected—only to find out as that his talent is the key to the troupes menacing plans for the future.

A thief steals a magical artifact that allows him to manipulate memories. As he goes deeper into the memories of the wealthy people he steals from, he uncovers a conspiracy that shakes the foundations of their entire world. He must race against time, and himself, to stop what's coming.

In a dystopian future, a street vagrant plans the greatest heist of all time—the key to Arcadia, the city of dreams. He pulls off the daring entry to the sacred space, only to find something inside that will forever change his life, and the future itself.

A villain from one of your favorite books or movie has somehow escaped his world and come into yours. He has already scorched a trail of disaster and is headed to find you. Now, you must find a way to battle his powers in a world that has none—or so you think.

A physician's apprentice discovers that the treatments that seem to cure all of his patients has really been coming from an otherworldly place. When it comes to the apprentice's time to learn the art of healing from his mentor, he is shocked at what he finds out.

In a city where the shadows come to life from a malevolent curse, a shy artist must brave the daylight to find the cavern by the sea rumored to hold the clue to setting the town free. Can the gentle young artist survive her own shadows that seem to have a secret of their own?

Write a fan fiction story using one of your favorite main characters. However, in this alternate storyline, the main character is really the villain. Start from anywhere in the existing storyline or make up an entirely new one but your beloved character must be treacherous.

Beneath the surface of a peaceful countryside lies a network of caves filled with mysterious waters. A lonely young farmer, filled with dreams of something bigger, stumbles into a cavern and when he steps into the water, something happens that will forever change him.

After a near-drowning accident, a teen discovers they can breathe underwater. Afraid to tell anyone, they sneak off to explore the depths around their coastal town. They are thrilled to find a whole new world under the sea, until they make a troubling discovery.

Take any story that happened in real life, to you or one you heard about, and turn it into a fictional story set in a fantasy realm. Turn modern conveniences into magical powers and people or animals into fantastical beings.

A blacksmith discovers a fallen star and forges a blade of unparalleled power. The star's essence grants the weapon the ability to cut through the fabric of reality. When the blacksmith becomes a target for those who crave the blade's power he must find a way to destroy it before it can destroy everything else.

A mapmaker discovers a series of floating islands high above the clouds. The islands harbor a civilization that keeps a terrible secret. When the mapmaker figures out just how terrible that secret is, he races to keep his new discovery from the rest of the world.

An orphaned castle maid barely survives with little sleep and food rations barely fit for an animal. Faint with exhaustion and hunger, she eats the leftovers from the reclusive queen's plate. What happens immediately after is a story of magical proportions.

Teenage twins find a map tucked in an old book that was abandoned on a park bench. The map reveals not a fixed location but a shifting nexus of dimensions. When one twin disappears leaving only some cryptic notes written on the map 's margins, their twin must decipher the notes and find out which alternate reality they are lost in and how they will both get back alive.

And So It Begins...

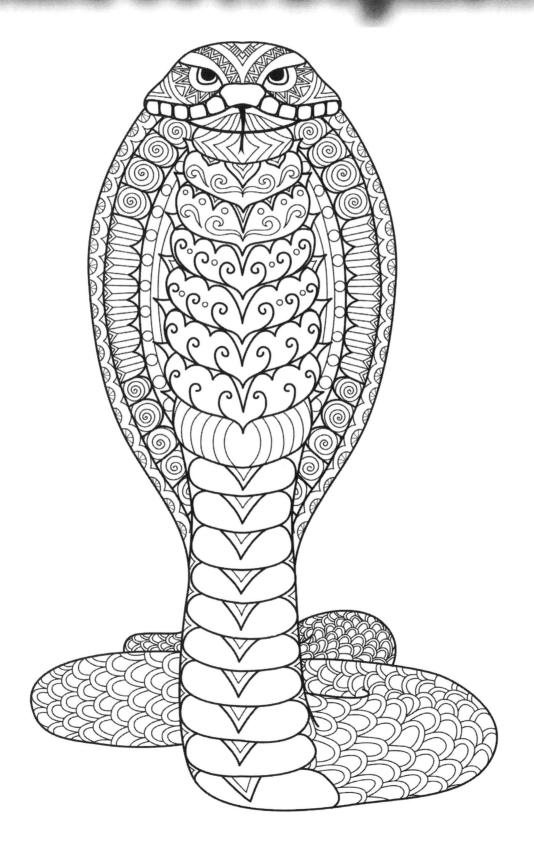

STORY RESEARCH

Research Topic _____

Notes

KEY INFORMATION

STATISTICS & DATA

LANGUAGE & SLANG

Website Resources Used

_____

WORLDBUILDING

Location _____

Brief Description

What are the people/Culture like?

How is the climate & Terrain

Describe using 5 senses

What do people do all day?

Website Resources Used

_____

_____

Notes

_____

_____

CHARACTER

Character Name _____

SKETCH OR PASTE IMAGE

NickName _____

Physical Description

_____
_____
_____
_____
_____

Personality

_____
_____
_____
_____
_____

POSITIVE IDEALS

NEGATIVE IDEALS

Habits / Quirks

_____
_____
_____
_____

GOALS AND MOTIVATIONS

Background

_____
_____
_____
_____

CHARACTER

Character Name _____

SKETCH OR PASTE IMAGE

NickName _____

Physical Description

_____
_____
_____
_____
_____
_____

POSITIVE IDEALS

Personality

_____
_____
_____
_____
_____

NEGATIVE IDEALS

Habits / Quirks

_____
_____
_____
_____

GOALS AND MOTIVATIONS

Background

_____
_____
_____
_____

CONFLICT

Who is the Conflict between?

Why are they having this conflict?

How does the character react internally?

How does the character react externally?

How is the conflict resolved?

How does the character change from this conflict?

How does the conflict affect the story?

STORY TIMELINE

Story Title:

Research Topic _____

Notes

KEY INFORMATION

_____
_____
_____
_____
_____
_____

STATISTICS & DATA

_____
_____
_____
_____
_____
_____
_____
_____

LANGUAGE & SLANG

_____
_____
_____
_____
_____
_____

Website Resources Used

_____   _____

WORLDBUILDING

Location _____

BRIEF DESCRIPTION

WHAT ARE THE PEOPLE/CULTURE LIKE?

HOW IS THE CLIMATE & TERRAIN

DESCRIBE USING 5 SENSES

WHAT DO PEOPLE DO ALL DAY?

Website Resources Used

_____

_____

Notes

_____

_____

CHARACTER

Character Name _____

SKETCH OR PASTE IMAGE

NickName _____

Physical Description

_____
_____
_____
_____
_____

Personality

_____
_____
_____
_____
_____

POSITIVE IDEALS

NEGATIVE IDEALS

Habits / Quirks

_____
_____
_____
_____

GOALS AND MOTIVATIONS

Background

_____
_____
_____
_____

CHARACTER

Character Name _____

Sketch or Paste Image

NickName _____

Physical Description

_____
_____
_____
_____

Positive Ideals

Personality

_____
_____
_____
_____

Negative Ideals

Habits / Quirks

_____
_____
_____

Goals and Motivations

Background

_____
_____
_____

CONFLICT

Who is the Conflict between?

Why are they having this conflict?

How does the character react internally?

How does the character react externally?

How is the conflict resolved?

How does the character change from this conflict?

How does the conflict affect the story?

STORY TIMELINE

Story Title:

STORY RESEARCH

Research Topic _____

Notes

KEY INFORMATION

STATISTICS & DATA

LANGUAGE & SLANG

Website Resources Used

_____

WORLDBUILDING

Location _____

BRIEF DESCRIPTION

WHAT ARE THE PEOPLE/CULTURE LIKE?

HOW IS THE CLIMATE & TERRAIN

DESCRIBE USING 5 SENSES

WHAT DO PEOPLE DO ALL DAY?

Website Resources Used

_____

_____

Notes

_____

_____

CHARACTER

Character Name _____

SKETCH OR PASTE IMAGE

NickName _____

Physical Description

_____
_____
_____
_____
_____

Personality

_____
_____
_____
_____

POSITIVE IDEALS

NEGATIVE IDEALS

Habits / Quirks

_____
_____
_____
_____

GOALS AND MOTIVATIONS

Background

_____
_____
_____
_____

CHARACTER

Character Name _____

SKETCH OR PASTE IMAGE

NickName _____

Physical Description

_____
_____
_____
_____
_____

POSITIVE IDEALS

Personality

_____
_____
_____
_____
_____
_____

NEGATIVE IDEALS

Habits / Quirks

_____
_____
_____
_____

GOALS AND MOTIVATIONS

Background

_____
_____
_____
_____

CONFLICT

Who is the Conflict between?

Why are they having this conflict?

How does the character react internally?

How does the character react externally?

How is the conflict resolved?

How does the character change from this conflict?

How does the conflict affect the story?

STORY TIMELINE

Story Title:

STORY RESEARCH

Research Topic _____

Notes

KEY INFORMATION

STATISTICS & DATA

LANGUAGE & SLANG

Website Resources Used

_____

WORLDBUILDING

Location _____

Brief Description

What are the people/Culture like?

How is the climate & Terrain

Describe using 5 senses

What do people do all day?

Website Resources Used

Notes

CHARACTER

Character Name _____

SKETCH OR PASTE IMAGE

NickName _____

Physical Description

_____
_____
_____
_____
_____
_____

POSITIVE IDEALS

Personality

_____
_____
_____
_____

NEGATIVE IDEALS

Habits / Quirks

_____
_____
_____

GOALS AND MOTIVATIONS

Background

_____
_____
_____
_____

CHARACTER

Character Name _____

SKETCH OR PASTE IMAGE

NickName _____

Physical Description

_____
_____
_____
_____
_____

POSITIVE IDEALS

Personality

_____
_____
_____
_____

NEGATIVE IDEALS

Habits / Quirks

_____
_____
_____
_____

GOALS AND MOTIVATIONS

Background

_____
_____
_____
_____

CONFLICT

Who is the Conflict between?	
Why are they having this conflict?	
How does the character react internally?	
How does the character react externally?	
How is the conflict resolved?	
How does the character change from this conflict?	
How does the conflict affect the story?	

STORY TIMELINE

Story Title:

STORY RESEARCH

Research Topic _____

KEY INFORMATION

Notes

_____
_____
_____
_____
_____
_____
_____

STATISTICS & DATA

_____
_____
_____
_____
_____
_____
_____

LANGUAGE & SLANG

_____
_____
_____
_____
_____

Website Resources Used _____

_____ _____

WORLDBUILDING

Location _____

BRIEF DESCRIPTION

WHAT ARE THE PEOPLE/CULTURE LIKE?

HOW IS THE CLIMATE & TERRAIN

DESCRIBE USING 5 SENSES

WHAT DO PEOPLE DO ALL DAY?

Website Resources Used

_____

_____

Notes

_____

_____

CHARACTER

Character Name _____

SKETCH OR PASTE IMAGE

NickName _____

Physical Description

_____

_____

_____

_____

Personality

POSITIVE IDEALS

_____

_____

_____

_____

NEGATIVE IDEALS

Habits / Quirks

_____

_____

_____

_____

GOALS AND MOTIVATIONS

Background

_____

_____

_____

_____

CHARACTER

Character Name _____

SKETCH OR PASTE IMAGE

NickName _____

Physical Description

_____
_____
_____
_____
_____

Personality

_____
_____
_____
_____
_____

POSITIVE IDEALS

NEGATIVE IDEALS

Habits / Quirks

_____
_____
_____
_____
_____

GOALS AND MOTIVATIONS

Background

_____
_____
_____
_____
_____

CONFLICT

Who is the Conflict between?

Why are they having this conflict?

How does the character react internally?

How does the character react externally?

How is the conflict resolved?

How does the character change from this conflict?

How does the conflict affect the story?

STORY TIMELINE

Story Title:

STORY RESEARCH

Research Topic _____

Notes

KEY INFORMATION

STATISTICS & DATA

LANGUAGE & SLANG

Website Resources Used

_____

WORLDBUILDING

Location _____

BRIEF DESCRIPTION

WHAT ARE THE PEOPLE/CULTURE LIKE?

HOW IS THE CLIMATE & TERRAIN

DESCRIBE USING 5 SENSES

WHAT DO PEOPLE DO ALL DAY?

Website Resources Used

_____

_____

Notes

_____

_____

CHARACTER

Character Name _____

SKETCH OR PASTE IMAGE

NickName _____

Physical Description

_____

_____

_____

_____

Personality

_____

_____

_____

_____

_____

POSITIVE IDEALS

NEGATIVE IDEALS

Habits / Quirks

_____

_____

_____

_____

GOALS AND MOTIVATIONS

Background

_____

_____

_____

_____

CHARACTER

Character Name _____

SKETCH OR PASTE IMAGE

NickName _____

Physical Description

_____
_____
_____
_____
_____
_____

POSITIVE IDEALS

Personality

_____
_____
_____
_____
_____
_____

NEGATIVE IDEALS

Habits / Quirks

_____
_____
_____
_____

GOALS AND MOTIVATIONS

Background

_____
_____
_____
_____

CONFLICT

Who is the Conflict between?

Why are they having this conflict?

How does the character react internally?

How does the character react externally?

How is the conflict resolved?

How does the character change from this conflict?

How does the conflict affect the story?

STORY TIMELINE

Story Title:

_____

_____

_____

_____

_____

_____

_____

_____

_____

_____

_____

_____

_____

_____

_____

_____

_____

_____

_____

_____

_____

_____

STORY RESEARCH

Research Topic _____

Notes

KEY INFORMATION

STATISTICS & DATA

LANGUAGE & SLANG

Website Resources Used

_____

WORLDBUILDING

Location _____

BRIEF DESCRIPTION

WHAT ARE THE PEOPLE/CULTURE LIKE?

HOW IS THE CLIMATE & TERRAIN

DESCRIBE USING 5 SENSES

WHAT DO PEOPLE DO ALL DAY?

Website Resources Used

_____

_____

Notes

_____

_____

CHARACTER

Character Name _____

SKETCH OR PASTE IMAGE

NickName _____

Physical Description

_____
_____
_____
_____

Personality

_____
_____
_____
_____

POSITIVE IDEALS

NEGATIVE IDEALS

Habits / Quirks

_____
_____
_____

GOALS AND MOTIVATIONS

Background

_____
_____
_____

CHARACTER

Character Name _____

SKETCH OR PASTE IMAGE

NickName _____

Physical Description

_____
_____
_____
_____
_____

POSITIVE IDEALS

Personality

_____
_____
_____
_____

NEGATIVE IDEALS

Habits / Quirks

_____
_____
_____
_____

GOALS AND MOTIVATIONS

Background

_____
_____
_____
_____

CONFLICT

Who is the Conflict between?

Why are they having this conflict?

How does the character react internally?

How does the character react externally?

How is the conflict resolved?

How does the character change from this conflict?

How does the conflict affect the story?

STORY TIMELINE

Story Title:

Bonus Worksheets

STORY RESEARCH

Research Topic _____

KEY INFORMATION

Notes

_____

_____

_____

_____

_____

_____

STATISTICS & DATA

_____

_____

_____

_____

_____

_____

_____

_____

LANGUAGE & SLANG

_____

_____

_____

_____

_____

_____

Website Resources Used

_____

_____   _____

WORLDBUILDING

Location _____

Brief Description

What are the people/Culture like?

How is the climate & Terrain

Describe using 5 senses

What do people do all day?

Website Resources Used

Notes

_____

_____

CHARACTER

Character Name _____

SKETCH OR PASTE IMAGE

NickName _____

Physical Description

_____
_____
_____
_____

POSITIVE IDEALS

Personality

_____
_____
_____
_____

NEGATIVE IDEALS

Habits / Quirks

_____
_____
_____

GOALS AND MOTIVATIONS

Background

_____
_____
_____

CHARACTER

Character Name _____

SKETCH OR PASTE IMAGE

NickName _____

Physical Description

_____
_____
_____
_____
_____

Personality

_____
_____
_____
_____
_____

POSITIVE IDEALS

NEGATIVE IDEALS

Habits / Quirks

_____
_____
_____
_____

GOALS AND MOTIVATIONS

Background

_____
_____
_____
_____

CONFLICT

Who is the Conflict between?

Why are they having this conflict?

How does the character react internally?

How does the character react externally?

How is the conflict resolved?

How does the character change from this conflict?

How does the conflict affect the story?

STORY TIMELINE

STORY RESEARCH

Research Topic _____

Notes

KEY INFORMATION

STATISTICS & DATA

LANGUAGE & SLANG

Website Resources Used

_____

WORLDBUILDING

Location _____

BRIEF DESCRIPTION

WHAT ARE THE PEOPLE/CULTURE LIKE?

HOW IS THE CLIMATE & TERRAIN

DESCRIBE USING 5 SENSES

WHAT DO PEOPLE DO ALL DAY?

Website Resources Used

_____

_____

Notes

_____

_____

CHARACTER

Character Name _____

SKETCH OR PASTE IMAGE

NickName _____

Physical Description

_____
_____
_____
_____
_____

Personality

_____
_____
_____
_____
_____

POSITIVE IDEALS

NEGATIVE IDEALS

Habits / Quirks

_____
_____
_____
_____

GOALS AND MOTIVATIONS

Background

_____
_____
_____
_____

CHARACTER

Character Name _____

SKETCH OR PASTE IMAGE

NickName _____

Physical Description

_____
_____
_____
_____
_____
_____

POSITIVE IDEALS

Personality

_____
_____
_____
_____
_____
_____

NEGATIVE IDEALS

Habits / Quirks

_____
_____
_____
_____
_____

GOALS AND MOTIVATIONS

Background

_____
_____
_____
_____
_____

CONFLICT

Who is the Conflict between?

Why are they having this conflict?

How does the character react internally?

How does the character react externally?

How is the conflict resolved?

How does the character change from this conflict?

How does the conflict affect the story?

STORY TIMELINE

About the Author

Jane Garrett is the pen name for Sarah Reid. Why a pen name? Not to have a secret identity or escape a life of crime. She's not that exciting. No, her pen name is much more personal.

Sarah chose that name many years ago when she dreamed of becoming a full-time author. She wanted her author's persona to reflect the family effort it takes to support someone who chooses a career in writing.

Her mom, also her biggest fan, lost her battle with breast cancer in 2012. Sarah and her mom share the same middle name, Jane. Her amazing husband, Captain Awesome, also known as Garrett to mere mortals, encouraged her for many years to pursue this path. Patience is his superpower. Sarah is now a full-time author and Jane Garrett represents the support system that helped get her there.

Sarah obtained her BA in Organizational Management from the University of Arizona GC and her MA in Writing from Johns Hopkins University. She homeschooled her two children through high school graduation before sending them off to college. Her son has a BA in graphic design and studio art from Liberty University and is the illustrator for all her books. Her daughter has her BA in English from Maryville University and teaches creative writing for Kids Write Novels, a division of Innovative Learning Press.

Sarah has written ten curriculum books and two kids fiction books as well as several short stories. In April of 2021, she started her own publishing company, Innovative Learning Press with a desire to bring more engaging and helpful curriculum to students around the country. As an author and teacher, Jane Garrett is passionate about helping students be involved and intentional when making choices for their future. Her writing focuses on helping young people find their own passion for learning.

Books by Jane Garrett

Non-Fiction

180 Days to Save the World: Young Adult (9-12th grades)

180 Days to Save the World: Short Story (6-12th grades)

180 Days to Save the World: Middle Grade (6-8th grades)

180 Days to Save the World: Chapter Book (4-5th grades)

180 Days to Save the World: Creative Writing (2-3rd grades)

180 Days to Save the World: Graphic Novel (6-12th grades)

The Art of Tiny Tales: Flash Fiction

The Art of Observation: Description Journaling for Authors

The Encephalon Code: Level 1 (7-8th grades)

The Encephalon Code: Level 2 (9-10th grades)

The Encephalon Code: Level 3 (11-12th grades)

Fiction

Remy & Finn: Mischief in the Meadow

A Colonial Kidnapping

Follow Us on Social Media

 https://www.facebook.com/Innovativelearningpress

 https://www.instagram.com/kidswritenovels/

 https://www.pinterest.com/InnovativeLearningPress

Made in the USA
Columbia, SC
20 March 2025

55434642R00076